My skin is dark like the cocao

beans in the big brown sack.

I love my beige skin tone

Oh hey!

My name is Jack!

My skin color is so sweet and pure

just like the honey that's on the rack.

I am brown like this delicious chocolate

that I am having for a snack.

Fair-skinned is my color

mixed with many shades of black.

My skin is the color of the beautiful

sand on the beach that i'm going to stack.

My skin matches the color

that is on the running track.

EE DOLLS

HONEY POTS

TIPS

HONE

Melanin-Rich is what I call myself.

My beauty in matches my beauty out

and there's nothing that I lack.

We all have different skin shades,

but we are all unique.

Love yourself and friends around you

because we are all amazing.

Always remember that you are beautiful

inside and out, no matter what.

No one can change your lovely heart.

your skin, my dear, is a work of art.

My skin

Your skin

Our skin

All skin

CAN YOU FIND YOUR SKIN TONE?

Children's Affirmation:

I AM BEAUTIFUL

I AM SMART

I AM STRONG

I AM HAPPY

I AM ENOUGH

MY SKIN TONE
DOES NOT DEFINE ME.

I AM BRAVE

I AM KIND

I AM LOVED

I AM A GREAT FRIEND

I AM WHO I AM

Made in United States
Orlando, FL
11 July 2024

48804871R00015